SUGAR, SUGAR

SUGARED AND SPICED
BOOK ONE

LADY MARIE

CONTENTS

To me, myself, and I.
Because one was never going to be enough.

CONTENT WARNING

This may be a short read, but it packs a big punch. It explores sugar daddy/sugar baby relationships and features graphic sexual content. If you think either of these things aren't for you, it may be a good idea to skip this novella.

1

SAGE

BENJAMIN:

Are you available this evening?

I STARED DOWN AT THE WORDS THAT HAD COME through about fifteen minutes ago while I was still on the massage table. I needed a little time to turn his request over in my mind.

On the one hand, now that my last spa service of the day was finished, my plan entailed going home and settling down with a glass of wine or two and takeout from my favorite tapas restaurant while watching one of my favorite nineties movies, *In Too Deep*. Today had been all about decompressing. While I might not regret my decision to go back to school for my master's degree at this stage in my life, I didn't realize just how exhausted, both mentally and physically, the decision would leave me. It'd been a rough week of trying to make classes and deadlines, and I'd been looking forward to using today strictly for relaxation.

On the other hand, an evening with Benjamin Jordan never disappointed—in terms of both quality and the effect on my wallet. The bi-weekly direct deposits he made into my account were always generous and right on time. In fact, it was on his dime that I'd been able to pamper myself today. Going on a last-minute date might just be the perfect thank you for his contribution. But I wasn't ready to agree that easily.

> What did you have in mind?

As much as I enjoyed his company, if I was going to be giving up my night of peace and solitude, I needed to know what I was getting myself into. Especially since it was so rare for him to reach out on short notice like this.

BENJAMIN:

Nothing extravagant. One of my close friends is having a soft opening for his boutique hotel downtown. Nothing big or over the top.

> How soft are we talking?

BENJAMIN:

No more than twenty-five people. Maybe thirty.

That was definitely outside of the usual scope of the events that Benji took me to. It wasn't uncommon for me to be his plus-one. That was the whole premise of our arrangement, but they were always large-scale. The only exceptions were the few vacations we'd gone on, just the two of us, but even those had some sort of business component to them. Casual, intimate gatherings weren't exactly something we'd done before.

Nibbling on my bottom lip, I thought about what he was asking. When I decided to explore this sugar daddy/sugar baby dynamic, I had very clear expectations and desires. I may have been looking for an older man, but that didn't mean I was looking for someone who was old and crusty. A bit of gray was just fine because I'd always loved the distinguished look on a man. Someone with money was also a requirement, obviously, because working full-time while going to school was just not the sort of stress that I needed in my life right now. I wanted someone who would be able to fund the lifestyle that I wanted without making me feel controlled, demeaned, or uneasy. And to round my request out, I wanted someone who understood boundaries. *That* was an absolute non-negotiable. Dates when you need someone to accompany you to high-scale events, a vacation companion, the occasional dinner a few times a month. Those were all things I was willing to do. I was *not*, however, trying to get paid by a creep who felt like his money entitled him to my body.

Not many men understood that when I first signed up for Sugared and Spiced. It was considered an upscale and discreet service, complete with background checks and exclusive membership that required invitations and referrals. Their vetting process was pretty thorough, and they took safety seriously, which meant that creeps were either non-existent or discarded as soon as they were discovered. Even so, the majority of the men I connected with in the beginning were very clear that sex was part of the package that they were looking for.

One of the reasons that Benjamin stood out from all the rest was because, much like me, he wasn't looking for someone to satisfy his physical needs. He also wasn't trying to find someone to play the role of his girlfriend, which was a definite plus. He simply wanted to have a companion who he could spoil whenever he wanted to and a gorgeous date on his arm when necessary. Benji always respected my time, asking for my company and never demanding it. He took an interest in my life, taking the things that I enjoyed into account, and made sure to pay attention when I talked about school or family. There were countless times over the last year when he not only helped me stay focused but offered a shoulder to lean on and a listening ear whenever I needed it. If I couldn't accompany him on a date, he never fussed, threw a tantrum, or threatened to withhold money from me. Hell, a couple of months into our arrangement, I'd told Benji that I wouldn't be able to go out of town with him to his business partner's gala because I had an exam coming up that required all of my attention. He wouldn't even hear my suggestion to cancel the deposit he had scheduled for the next week and was genuinely offended that I'd even thought it. If you looked up the phrase 'perfect gentleman' in the dictionary, Benji's picture would be there, front and center.

I could honestly say that we'd become something akin to friends during our time together. He was sweet, caring, accommodating, and could charm anybody in any room. Whenever we were together, I was constantly in awe. We flirted, of course, but it never crossed into uncomfortable or dangerous territory. The time we spent together was genuinely enjoyable, and it never felt like an obligation or something I was paid to do, even though it obviously was. So, while I didn't get the impression that this text had less than savory undertones, it definitely wasn't within our usual purview of agreed-upon interactions. Did I really want to blur the lines and step out of our box?

My response must have taken longer than I thought because soon, another message was coming through.

BENJAMIN:

Feel free to say no if it makes you uncomfortable. The thought crossed my mind that you might enjoy a bit of a break from the usual. I know your schedule has been a bit overwhelming for you this week and you might enjoy yourself, that's all.

I smiled at the fact that he was only proving my point about being a considerate gentleman. Just knowing that this invitation came from a genuine place of wanting to help me relax and have a bit of fun after a rough week had me ready to melt. It also didn't hurt that Benjamin was as fine as they came. Moments like these reminded me that my attraction to him was a very real thing, and even though we'd never crossed that line, I couldn't deny that Benji just did something to me. Would accepting his offer blur that line even more?

I thought about it, weighing my options. A quiet

night at home or a fun night out with the perfect eye candy, the type that was both fine and rich as hell...

Yeah, now that I really thought about it, this wasn't a difficult decision at all.

Fuck it.

I'd love to.

BENJAMIN:

Perfect. I'll send the car for you. Be ready by 6:30.

2

SAGE

At six-thirty on the dot, a call came through from the concierge of my building, letting me know that my car had arrived. That wasn't surprising. One of the most consistent things about Benjamin was that he was punctual. When we'd first met, he'd been adamant that lack of punctuality was one of his biggest pet peeves. Of course, being on time was something that I still hadn't mastered, but he took it in stride. He grumbled, and he teased, but his complaints were typically made in jest and usually whispered in my ear in the place of sweet nothings whenever we were in a crowd. There was also the added bonus that he always sent a car for me a bit early, just in case.

"Hey, Fran," I said, approaching the car, a genuine smile on my face. Francis was my usual driver for all things involving Benjamin. When Benjamin first started sending cars for me, I'd mentioned how much I enjoyed the older man's company, and sweetheart that he was, Benji made a point to put him on my regular detail.

"You know I hate it when you call me that," he responded with a sigh as he opened the back door of the town car for me. He tried to act like a grump, but I knew he secretly loved me to bits.

"Are you sure about that? Sounds false to me," I teased.

He grumbled something in response, but I didn't pay him any mind. I noticed the ghost of a smile that always appeared whenever I used the affectionate nickname.

Between traffic and distance, it took almost an hour for us to get to the hotel, but scrolling through social media and texting my cousin Alaina helped pass the time quickly. She was the only person who knew about Benjamin and our arrangement, mainly because, as my cousin and best friend, I knew there was no way she'd judge me. You'd think that considering I was thirty years old, I'd be free to live my own life and do as I pleased without comments from the peanut gallery, but with how nosey my family was, that was a lot easier said than done. Explaining to them that I was the paid non-sexual companion of a fifty-two-year-old businessman? Yeah, no way in hell was I getting out of that conversation unscathed.

"Will I be seeing you in a few hours, Fran?" I asked as we pulled up to our destination, Honey and Ivy Hotel.

He huffed. "I'd imagine so. Behave." We caught each other's eyes in the rearview mirror.

"Always," I said with a wink as a valet, who barely looked old enough to drink, opened the door and helped me out of the car.

I couldn't help but giggle as his young ass did a

double take. Yeah, I was definitely turning heads tonight in a form-fitting knee-length red sequined cocktail dress that not only showed a ridiculous amount of cleavage but exposed my back as well, thanks to the corset-style ribbon. My straightened dark hair was pulled up into a high ponytail, revealing the back of my dress, and I'd left a few strands out so that they'd fall in a way that framed my face. The facial and body treatment at the spa had my rich umber skin glowing, and I'd kept the makeup to a minimum on purpose, only playing up my naturally long lashes and full lips. Add to all that the fact that this dress made both my slim five-foot-six frame and my thick ass look amazing and there was no doubt in my mind that I looked damn good—and everyone around me would know it, too.

The valet wasn't the only one pumping my head up as I made my way through the front doors. The few people in the lobby of the hotel all turned, the heels of my gold red bottoms echoing against the tile and announcing my presence every step of the way. Only one person was actually worth my notice, though, and my eyes zeroed in on him almost immediately. At five foot ten, Benjamin may not always be the tallest man in the room, but there was never any question about whether or not he commanded everyone's attention. Once they found me, those storm-gray eyes trapped and shocked me like a bolt of electricity, just like they always did.

Benjamin was...delicious. The word fit him perfectly. With his almond-toned skin, strong jaw, close cut, and almost completely silver beard, his face was a work of art. If I were a betting woman, I'd venture to guess that several people would agree that it would serve as the perfect seat—not that I would confirm or deny ever thinking about it that way. Every time I laid eyes on him, my pussy started to purr, even when I didn't want her to.

This wasn't a physical relationship, so vocalizing that sentiment wouldn't exactly serve me, especially since, as far as I could tell, he didn't have any interest in revising that part of our agreement. That didn't mean my nights weren't spent with my favorite fully charged vibrator as I fantasized about his strong hands gripping my waist, his toned washboard stomach pressed against mine, and my thighs framing his hips as he pushed into me over and over again, the face in question staring down and waiting for me to break. Nope, it just meant that I had to keep those thoughts to myself.

Whatever conversation he'd been having with the three men surrounding him came to a halt once I arrived at his side. Four sets of eyes traced the lines of my body, but only one gave me the same pleasure as a soft caress.

"Sage. You look—" there was a pause as his eyes met mine, "radiant." That may have been what his mouth said, but his eyes seemed to tell a different story. The same one that I'd just been thinking of.

"A day of self-care will do that for you," I said, accepting the soft kiss he placed on my cheek. "Thank you for your contribution to that, by the way." The words were whispered before he could pull away so that they would be for his ears only.

A strong hand settled on my lower back, and my body melted at the possibility that it might slide just a bit lower, even though I knew it wouldn't. Benjamin was nothing if not respectful.

"My pleasure," he whispered back with a smile. Turning to face his companions, he added in a louder voice, "You're familiar with Seth, of course, but do you remember Arthur?"

"Of course! We met at Benji's charity gala in December." Seth smiled, clearly happy to be recognized, while Arthur gave a quiet hello.

An unfamiliar, amused voice broke through the re-introduction. "Benji? You didn't tell me you had such a cute nickname, friend."

"That's because you can't call him that." I followed my statement with a raised eyebrow as I pressed myself into Benjamin's side. "I don't think we've met."

"Oh, certainly not. I'd remember someone as gorgeous as you, love. Besides, if we'd met before today, I can guarantee you'd be my date and not his." The two other men groaned while Benjamin just chuckled.

"The cocky asshole here is Philip. This hotel is his latest business venture," Benjamin said with a shake of his head.

"Oh, so *this* is the one?"

"And which one would that be?" Philip asked, intrigued.

"The one forced to walk in my Benji's shadow." My tone was so matter-of-fact that everyone froze for a moment before an echo of deep laughter flowed through the group.

"Oh, I like her." Philip beamed.

I felt the rumble in Benjamin's chest as he said, "Trust me. So do I."

3

BENJAMIN

ABSOLUTELY FUCKABLE.

There were no other words to describe how Sage looked in that dress. Was the damn thing painted on? I had to fight every instinct that told me to knock out any motherfucker in the room who couldn't tear their eyes away from her. It wasn't because I was some insecure, primitive asshole who couldn't handle having a beautiful date. It was more about the fact that they just simply didn't deserve to lay eyes on such a breathtaking woman. Hell, I barely deserved to be able to. I paid for the privilege time and time again because I *knew* that she was more than worth it. That was the bottom line. I'd never been so torn between wanting to show her off and wanting to keep her all to myself.

The fact that she had the audacity to look like a ten-course meal and be charming as fuck had me ready to fall to my knees and worship her with my mouth, hands, and the inconveniently heavy dick I had to fight to keep contained in my slacks.

The decision to invite Sage to be my plus-one was something I'd been wrestling with for the better part of two weeks. I'd known the event was coming, but because of how intimate it was, I wasn't sure if inviting her would be the appropriate thing to do. Despite all of the time we'd spent together over the last year, having her around so many of my friends felt different from anything we'd done so far. It left me feeling a bit exposed, to be honest.

As her laugh echoed from across the room at something Seth was saying, I lost focus on whatever the hell was coming out of Arthur's mouth. It didn't go unnoticed.

"You are fucked, my friend. Completely and truly."

I cut my eyes at him, letting loose a grunt as I sipped the cognac in my glass. The slight burn offered me a bit of comfort. "Shut it."

"Just saying. You're a lot worse off than you were when I saw you two together a couple months ago. She's literally got your dick in a chokehold."

I chuckled, finally tearing my eyes away from Sage long enough to catch the smug look on my longtime friend's face. "You don't know shit about my dick, Arthur."

"And I'm happy to keep it that way. This is just me saying that that beautiful woman over there has your nose wide open, and neither of you actually seems to realize it."

Throwing back the rest of the drink, I just shook my head. "Trust me, she might not, but I certainly do." Leaning against the bar to signal the bartender for another drink, I let out a sigh. "You know things aren't like that between us." Arthur was the only person who knew about my arrangement with Sage. He'd been very vocal that I was full of shit, especially after seeing us together.

"Maybe it should be." Anyone watching would have thought Arthur had grown three heads by the way that I was looking at him. He let out a snort. "Don't act like it's impossible."

"It is. Listen, she didn't sign up for all that extra shit. Our agreement is what it is, and I don't really have the right to ask her for anything more."

Sage was very clear from the beginning about what she was looking for. Being intimate had always been a strict line for her, and she'd let me know that from day one. In all honesty, it had been the same with me. When we'd first met, I'd let her know that I wasn't looking for someone to warm my bed but instead someone who could make certain events feel worthwhile and offer me great company. She told me how relieved she was to hear that after meeting several men who were looking for the opposite. Most sugaresque relationships involved sex and physical intimacy in some capacity, but that's not what I was on then. Truthfully, I wasn't sure if that's what I was on now. I just knew there was no denying the pull that I felt each and every time we were together.

"All I'm saying is that I see that hungry look you get when you're staring at her. There's no way that she hasn't seen it, too. It would probably be to your benefit to at least see if it's something she'd like to take a chance on sooner rather than later before someone else does."

Arthur tipped his glass in my direction and headed

off into the crowd after imparting those words of supposed wisdom. I turned, my eyes seeking Sage again, only to find that she was already watching me. If the look she was sending my way was any indication, Arthur might be right. Maybe it was time for me to see if she'd like to change things up a bit. At least for tonight.

4

SAGE

THIS WAS...DIFFERENT. USUALLY, WHENEVER I accompanied Benji to an event, he was reserved and professional, his energy subdued. He was Benjamin, not Benji, in every sense of the word. Even on vacations, while we always had a good time, he was usually relaxed in a way that still lent itself to the persona he wanted everyone else to see. Classy, sophisticated, and quiet. That was never a problem for me, and I typically followed his lead, making polite conversation, flashing smiles, and dropping the occasional joke to lighten the mood or move the conversation along. Slightly reserved Sage complimented professional Benjamin perfectly.

The man that I was with tonight was not the one that I was used to dealing with. This was *relaxed* Benji. The Benji who let loose amongst his friends without a care in the world. I'd never seen him smile this much and certainly had never heard him laugh this often. He was rarely without a drink in his hand, and though he wasn't gulping them down or throwing them back, he was sipping them a lot more frequently than usual. Maybe it was the atmosphere, the company of his friends, or the alcohol itself, but with his lids low and his shoulders relaxed the way they were, he was in his element. It was sexy, and I wasn't ashamed to say it made me wet as ever.

Over the last two hours, we'd made our rounds through the room, soaking up the energy and mingling with guests. Now, we found ourselves sharing a velvet green corner booth with Arthur, Philip, Seth, and Seth's wife, Melinda. Despite the fact that Melinda was the one talking, I found my eyes drifting to where Benjamin sat on my left. Even the way he was sitting gave off a certain energy. One arm draped across the back of my seat while his hand kept a light grip on the back of my neck, which he was stroking with his thumb. Those thick legs of his were spread apart, taking up enough space that my thigh was forced to press against his, even with my legs crossed. It felt like he was trying to touch me as much and as often as possible. I mean, it wasn't like we were strangers to physical touch, but we usually kept it to a minimum. If he kept this up, I was definitely going to end up addicted to the feel of him.

"Everything okay?" The deep timbre of his voice sent a shiver through me as my eyes flicked up to meet his.

"Of course," I said, a smile appearing on my face. "Why wouldn't it be?"

He leaned in a bit closer, causing me to become more aware of my breathing. The sight of his tongue gliding across his lips nearly sent me into a spiral.

"I'm just checking. You're mighty quiet. Just wanted to make sure you're comfortable." Leaning in a bit more, his lips brushed against my exposed shoulder. Okay, that was absolutely new behavior. Did he realize we were in a room full of people?

"Clearly not as comfortable as you seem to be," I giggled. "I don't think I've ever seen this side of you, Benji." My eyes darted to the other side of the booth to see if anyone was paying us any mind.

"There are quite a few sides of me that you haven't seen before, Sage."

Was it just me, or had his voice gotten thicker? Bringing my eyes back to him, I was struck by the intensity of his gaze. My hand reached over, settling on his thigh as his neat, manicured nails dug just a bit into my neck. Any control I thought I had at the moment disappeared, and I was positive that someone had heard the moan that'd made its way up from my chest. My nipples tightened, and I knew the corset top of my dress wasn't doing a damn thing to hide them from sight.

He looked like he wanted to say something else, but suddenly the heat behind his eyes dimmed, and he pulled back, clearing his throat.

"Benj–"

"I'm going to grab some air," he announced, sliding out of the booth and standing at the front of the table.

If tonight was a night of firsts, then the way he sped across to the door that led to the back patio definitely qualified. Had he just gotten caught up in the vibes and the liquor, or were we feeling the same pull? I wasn't sure. Not about the answer or whether or not I wanted to figure it out.

Arthur, Seth, and Melinda made their escapes from

the table as well to head to the bar and the dance floor, leaving me and Philip by ourselves, though the latter seemed to be engrossed in his phone. That left me to my own thoughts. They didn't stray far, turning over every word, touch, and moment that had passed between Benjamin and me over the course of the night. At some point, my gaze drifted out onto the patio, watching as he leaned across the railing, gazing up toward the night sky.

"You're staring."

A voice snapped me from my trance, and I turned to see that Philip had both put his phone away and closed the distance between us. It didn't make me uncomfortable, but I still made sure to slide over just a bit. Philip was nice and all, but that didn't mean I wanted him in my personal space, even if this was his event.

According to what I'd learned tonight, he'd purchased the Honey and Ivy two years before and decided to renovate it from top to bottom. Now that it was finished, he was ready to open but wanted to celebrate the accomplishment with some of his closest friends and investors first—a way to toast his success. I knew it was the type of thing plenty of people did, but Philip was still a bit too cocky for my liking.

"The only way for you to know that I was staring would be for you to be doing the same exact thing."

"Can you blame me? I don't think anyone in this room has taken their eyes away from you for more than a few minutes at a time. It's like looking directly into the sun."

I smirked. "Be careful. They say staring at the sun too long is dangerous."

"I've always liked to take risks," he chuckled.

After a few moments of silence, he continued. "All night, I've been doing my best to come up with just what exactly your relationship with *Benji*—oops, I'm sorry, Benjamin is."

"And what have you come up with?" Curiosity seemed to be taking over, both his and mine.

"I'm stumped. Benjamin has never had difficulty attracting beautiful women but forgive me if I'm curious about what exactly a man his age has to offer you. Other than money, that is."

His observation may have hit the nail on the head, but that didn't mean his assumption was any less offensive.

My attitude was clear in my response. "You know what they say about assuming things, don't you? And it appears to me that you've made the assumption that you know me."

"Not at all. Just saying what I'm sure you two have heard time and time again."

"Mmm, seems to me like you're projecting. You may not have anything else to offer women besides your money, but that doesn't mean that applies to everyone else."

"Touché," he said, clearly amused. "So, how about you set the record straight?"

"Not that it's any of your business, but Benjamin and I are just friends. Two people who happen to enjoy each other's company."

"Hmm, and how exactly does one become your... friend? Maybe even a slightly better friend than Benji?"

His light tone and easy smile kept most, but not all, of the ick factor out of his words. Still, I wasn't interested. Not in the slightest.

"Sorry. All slots are filled. I'm a booked and busy girl." A shrug followed my words before I turned, my eyes searching for my actual date. When they finally found him, it was clear that in the time I'd spent talking to Philip, Benjamin had found his own company.

And even though it wasn't necessary for him to comment on what I could see with my own eyes, Philip still felt the need to say, "Well, it looks like he has at least one slot open."

5

BENJAMIN

Being around Sage had never been this tempting or this difficult. I'd been attracted to her from the moment that we'd met but putting that attraction to the back of my mind was never an issue. So why the hell was it turning into a problem tonight? I was drawn to her over and over again, and it made me feel completely out of control. Coming outside and getting some fresh air was my attempt at putting some distance between us to help clear my head, but damn, it wasn't working. I could still smell her perfume, still feel the way my lips ghosted over her skin and how her body reacted to my grip on the back of her neck. Her moan was still ringing in my ears, and it was a sound that I wanted to hear on a constant loop.

Glancing back toward the table, I saw Philip sliding closer to Sage, that tell-tale smile on his face that said he was trying to make his move. Something pulled in my chest as I quickly looked away. Who the fuck did he think he was? We may have been friends, and this may have been his party, but that didn't mean he was entitled to flirt with my date right in front of me.

You're really pushing it tonight.

Yeah, well, I'd rather be pushing into her.

I couldn't help the chuckle that escaped me with that last thought. Nothing about the image was funny, but the thought that Sage would want to adjust our current boundaries to allow something like that was. No matter what her reactions were at the table or how much she flirted, that didn't mean she was starting to change her mind.

"Mind letting me in on the joke?"

The voice that said those words was familiar. Maybe a bit ill-timed, but not unwelcome. Maria found her way next to me, putting a face to the voice.

"Something tells me you wouldn't find my thoughts nearly as entertaining as I do. I'm sure history would agree with me."

"Yes, well, it's been a couple of years. Things may have changed." I gave her a knowing look, which only made both of us laugh. "At least a few things," she added.

I let my eyes travel over her, taking in her alluring appearance. "Well, I can confidently say one thing that hasn't changed is how amazing you look."

"Or how amazing we look together," she said pointedly.

Keeping the strain from my face was a challenge, to say the least. The last thing I wanted to do was play Maria's games tonight. We'd always been able to enjoy one another's company, evident by our three-year relationship, but in the end, we wanted different things. Staying friends wasn't difficult for us, mainly because we'd always run in similar circles, and avoiding one another just wasn't feasible, but if I was honest with myself, I'd been hoping she wouldn't be here tonight.

Fingers creeping up my arm pulled me from my thoughts, causing me to finally notice just how close Maria actually was. "If I remember correctly, we always *felt* amazing together, too."

"That was never our problem," I said, easing away from her to create some space between us.

"On that, we can definitely agree."

"That was also a while ago, Maria."

"Not *too* long ago," she responded coyly.

"Long enough." My voice was stern, an attempt to emphasize my point. It'd been two years since we'd been together that way, and I had no interest in revisiting that part of our relationship.

She appeared to have something else to add but stopped, her lips suddenly turned down in displeasure. The feel of a warm body pressing against my side and fingers sliding against mine until a hand with long, deep red-painted nails gripped my glass let me know the source of her sudden change in mood. I turned just in time to see Sage taking a sip of the dark liquid, her eyes never leaving Maria.

"I hope I'm not interrupting." That may have been what her mouth said, but the look on her face and her tone of voice told a different story. Interrupt was exactly what she'd set out to do. She wasn't about to get any complaints from me. Maria, on the other hand...

"Actually, we're in the middle of a private conversation."

Sage was clearly amused as she answered, "I'm so sorry." Turning her attention to me and swirling what was left of my drink in the glass, she said, "I was starting to miss you. Philip's company isn't nearly as captivating as yours."

"That doesn't surprise me at all," I smirked.

I couldn't take my eyes off Sage as she took another sip. Would the cognac taste any different if it came from her lips? There's no question that it would have to be better, right? The way she held my gaze suggested she was waiting for me to lean in and find out.

Maria clearing her throat finally broke the trance I'd found myself in. "Aren't you going to introduce me to your...*friend*, Benjamin?"

With a giggle, Sage held out her hand. "Benji can be so rude sometimes. He tends to get a bit distracted when I'm around. I'm Sage. And you are?"

"Maria." The one-word answer and very limp hand-shake spoke for themselves.

Moving so that she was now firmly in front of me, Sage smiled. As much as I should probably try to defuse this situation because I knew just how uncomfortable Maria could make it if she tried, I found myself pulling Sage's body back into mine instead. Maria's eyes didn't miss the movement.

"I had no idea you'd brought a date, Benjamin. I

certainly hope you plan on getting her home in time for curfew."

Before I could gather my response, Sage had her own.

"Oh, you don't have to worry about that. Benji is very well-versed in getting me to bed on time."

Thank God she'd finished off my drink because if I'd been taking a sip, I might have choked. The innuendo was clear, and I wasn't sure which caught me off guard more: the fact that Sage wanted Maria to think we were intimate or the picture of her lying on the bed for me, ready and waiting.

The steam coming from Maria's ears was nearly visible. She mumbled something about excusing herself and made a beeline back through the patio doors and into the party. As funny as the entire scene was, I silently hoped that she couldn't actually hear me laughing after she left.

Watching Sage as she turned around to face me, I said, "If I didn't know any better, I'd say you were a bit jealous." Something about that amused me. Maybe it was the fact that I'd felt just as off-balance watching Philip slide closer to her in that booth earlier.

"Let's just say I didn't really appreciate that she didn't seem to understand the concept of personal boundaries," Sage huffed. "Who was she, anyway?"

"My ex. We haven't been together in a few years."

"Hmmm...well, it seems like she didn't really get that memo. Hopefully, she got this one, though."

A chuckle loosed itself from my chest as I wrapped my arms around her waist, pulling her into me until our bodies pressed together again.

"I don't think I've ever seen this side of you," I said,

tossing the words she'd thrown my way back at her. "I quite enjoy territorial, slightly aggressive Sage. "

The way her eyes lowered as she traced her finger along my chest caused my dick to harden between us. We were almost eye level, so it didn't take much for me to see just how much heat her gaze held. "Trust me. You'll know when I'm being aggressive."

Instead of pulling away, I followed my instincts and allowed my lips to graze hers. She took the hint, taking charge of the kiss and moaning against me. My cognac really did taste so much fucking better on her lips.

Moving our bodies until she was pressed against the balcony, one hand held her neck while the other formed something close to a death grip on her hip. The not-so-subtle way she was grinding against me had me ready to hike her dress up right here and now.

As much as it pained me, I finally managed to break the kiss, my resolve just about shattering when Sage whimpered in protest.

"Sage, I—" Words failed me because what the fuck was I supposed to say? Should I tell her I wanted nothing more than to be buried in the slice of heaven between her legs, even though it went against the very parameters we'd set? Was I supposed to tell her just how much I wanted to have her ride my face so I could fully taste her?

Her perfectly arched eyebrows scrunched in what seemed to be frustration. "How much longer do we have to be here?"

"We can leave whenever you're ready." Had I fucked this up that bad? I knew I should've kept my fucking lips to my—

"Good. Because I need you to ask Philip for a room."

I know my face showed my surprise. Even with that request, nothing could've prepared me for what left her lips next.

"Unless you plan on fucking me right here on this patio for everyone to see."

6

SAGE

I<small>T WAS AMAZING HOW QUICKLY TONIGHT WENT</small> from a casual night of fun to a 'horny thoughts only' situation. Something about seeing ole girl in his face triggered something new inside of me. I wasn't a jealous or possessive woman by nature, or at least I'd never been before. It wasn't like I had a real claim on Benji, but if anyone was going to be smiling in his face like they wanted him to dick them down in the middle of this little shindig, it was going to be me.

Well, between the attraction you've been feeling since you met him and the fact that the only thing getting a taste of your sugar for the last year has been your favorite rose toy, this was bound to happen.

That had to be it. The sexual tension between us was nothing new, but it had never been this heightened. I'd gone home plenty of times after a date with Benjamin and pulled orgasm after orgasm from my body, thinking of his soft, casual touches and that sensual voice of his. It was all just finally boiling over. And if the way he told me to grab my things and meet him at the elevators before speeding off to find Philip was any sort of testimony, Benji was feeling the exact same thing.

As I waited, I pulled out my phone and scrolled down to Alaina's message thread. If I let her know what was happening, there was no question in my mind that she'd be screaming and egging me on. For months Alaina had been telling me to take him for a ride and test out the waters—her words, not mine. That was why I also knew that she'd be blowing up my phone, asking a ridiculous number of questions that I didn't necessarily have time to answer right now. Maybe I should wait. Shit, we might get to the room only for me to either chicken out or end up disappointed.

The decision on whether or not to send her a quick update was made for me when I heard a throat clear.

With a smirk on his face, Benjamin asked, "Trying to figure out who to call for a quick exit?" His tone was joking, but was I imagining things, or did he actually seem nervous about my answer?

"Not unless that's what you're hoping for. If you don't want me, then just say that," I joked right back.

The air between us changed as he stepped into my space. "The *only* thing I can think about right now is how much I want you, Sage."

His thumb traced over my bottom lip, my sole warning before we were kissing yet again. Why did he taste so goddamn good? Our tongues came together on a gasp, or maybe it was a moan. The sounds of the lobby turned to static, and I could only think about how he was kissing me like it was the last chance he'd ever have. I guess if we decided that this really was a one-night thing, then it would be. His hand ghosted down to the base of my throat, and the slight pressure he hit me with caused a flutter that went from my stomach all the way down to my clit.

A ding and then a tsking sound behind us ended the kiss too early for my liking. We hadn't even called for an elevator yet, but apparently, two older women had ridden it to our level and weren't too happy about the vision they saw once the doors opened.

"Can I help you?" I snapped, admittedly aggravated by their interruption.

One of them mumbled something that sounded suspiciously like "young girls being hot in the ass" as they moved past us. Before I could tell her exactly where to shove her opinions, Benjamin apologized and led me onto the elevator.

"Why would you apologize to them for me?! Her old ass ca—" There was no chance of me finishing whatever rant I'd been about to go on because as the doors began to close, my back was pushed against a wall, and that damn hand was back at the front of my throat as his lips crashed into mine.

I couldn't form a single thought that didn't have to do with what was happening right in this moment. The way his tongue tangled with mine put me in a trance. The kiss was the exact opposite of the mask he usually wore in public. It was hot and nasty, the shit wet dreams were made of. I could feel my thong being ruined by how turned on I was. Benjamin was a starved man looking for a meal, and my pussy wanted nothing more than to oblige. One of my legs wrapped around his hip on instinct as it pushed into my core, and it pulled every whine imaginable from my mouth. Each thrust pushed the front of my thong further into my sticky arousal and provided just the right amount of friction. I wanted more. *Needed* more. But the realization of where we were brought me to my senses. Or at least it tried to.

"The cameras," I gasped as his lips left mine and made their way down my neck. His tongue began tasting every inch of the skin there as he used the grip he still had on my throat to force my head to the side.

"Fuck 'em," he growled against my exposed skin.

No, fuck me was the thought that flitted across my mind, but I was saved from saying it aloud when the elevator dinged again, letting us know we'd arrived on our floor. The way he continued to attack my skin, most definitely leaving a mark, made it clear he really didn't care until "Benji..." escaped me on a moan.

He finally pulled away, and the lust-filled look he was giving me made it difficult to catch my breath. His chest heaved as he ran a hand across his face in what I could only assume was an attempt to calm himself down.

Clearing his throat and stepping in between the doors to prevent them from closing, all he said was, "Room 35." Well, shit...yes, sir.

7

BENJAMIN

I was losing it. Or maybe this was me finally coming to my senses. It wasn't exactly clear which was responsible for my behavior in the elevator, but as I watched Sage's hips sway during the walk to the corner suite, I realized I didn't really give a shit why my restraint had decided to disappear. I wanted this. I wanted *her*. As long as she felt the same, my mission for the rest of the night was to ensure that this was well worth both our time.

As we reached the suite, and I pulled the key from my pocket, it was hard to miss how quiet Sage had become. Sending a quick look her way, I opened the door and allowed her to enter the room first. No matter what she might think after my little show of aggression back there, I was still a gentleman.

Something about the silence after we crossed the threshold made the click of the door behind us that much louder.

"If—" "I'm—"

We laughed at both of us trying to talk at once.

"Ladies first."

She smiled before starting over. "I'm...umm...going to freshen up in the bathroom."

"Of course." I nodded, gesturing toward the bedroom of the suite, where I was sure she'd find the master bathroom. As she headed in that direction, it was near impossible not to tear my eyes away from her. I'd never failed to notice how voluptuous Sage was, but the vision of her ass as she walked away from me had my dick ready to stage a breakout.

"Get ahold of yourself," I hissed once I heard the bathroom door close. My hands gripped the edge of the bar counter, but that only made me think of the way she'd reacted to me when I was gripping her neck.

After a few deep breaths, I made my way into the bedroom and out onto the balcony. The spectacular view was a testament to why Philip had invested so much money into the property. I was proud of my friend. It was almost enough to make up for the ribbing he'd given me when I'd asked how quickly he could secure a room for the night.

❧

"I NEED A ROOM, PHILIP."

"Have a bit too much to drink there, Benjamin? Gotta say, you've never been a lightweight, but I guess old age caught up with you." He laughed at his own joke, causing me to roll my eyes.

"Philip." I wasn't sure what he saw in my face, but whatever it was brought a twinkle to his eye.

"Oh, you sly dog! I knew you two weren't just friends," he snickered.

I kicked myself and tried to rein in my frustration. "I don't care what you think you know, Phil. Fuck it." If I called Francis now, he could probably make pretty good time in getting here to pick us up. He could just take us back to my condo and—

"Wait, wait, wait," Philip managed to say between his chuckles. "Of course, I'll help you out. I set aside a few rooms just for the occasion. Well, not this occasion, but..." He shrugged. "Come on."

I was skeptical but followed him as he led me to the back office. It only took a few moments for him to grab a key and work the magic needed to get me a room. Just as I was making my way out, he said, "Hold on now, you're forgetting something."

I raised an eyebrow at the small box of condoms he pulled out of the bottom drawer of his desk, and his only response was, "You're welcome." I thought about asking him who the hell he planned on spending the night with but decided it wasn't really my business. Besides, I had a beautiful woman to get back to.

"Have fun," he called after me. I knew he was never going to let me hear the end of this, but I couldn't bring myself to mind.

"It's gorgeous," Sage said, her uncharacteristically shy voice reaching my ears and snapping me out of my thoughts.

Her silent approach caught me off guard, but the sight of her was what knocked the wind out of me. She was barefoot now, which explained why I hadn't heard her step out of the suite. The lipstick that had been kissed away was reapplied perfectly, and her face had a dewy glow. That ponytail of hers was begging to be wrapped up in my fist.

"Not even half as gorgeous as you."

The smirk that I'd come to love so much appeared. "Damn, Benji. I know I look good, but you've already got me up to the room. Lay it on too thick, and it may start going to a girl's head."

Her feet carried her over to me, and I welcomed her with open arms. Without her shoes, I'd gained a few inches in terms of a height advantage, but not much. "If anyone is going to get a big head out of this experience, it's more than likely going to be me."

"I guess that's true, especially since I can actually *feel* the big head in question." Her snickers were met with my groan.

"You know that's not what I meant. Now I feel like a pervy old man."

"Awww, sorry, Benji." She gave me what I was pretty sure was a fake pout. "Want a kiss to make it better?"

"Only if you really want to give me one."

She leaned up slightly, placing a soft kiss on my lips before pulling away. Her kisses were addicting. As soon as she was gone, I found myself leaning in for another, and she happily obliged. Before either of us could get too caught up, I pulled away.

"Something wrong?" The look on her face told me that she was clearly confused.

"As amazing as what we started downstairs..."

"And in the elevator," she added with a giggle.

"Yes, and in the elevator." I chuckled. "As amazing as what we started felt, I just want to make sure you want this. This isn't exactly what we...agreed on, so if you've changed your mind, I want you to let me know." Placing a finger under her chin to ensure she was looking at me, I said, "I'd never want to put you in an uncomfortable position, Sage."

Could she hear the sound of my dick cussing me out? I damn sure could. There was no doubt in my mind that if she said yes, I would be all in, at least for the night. Before that could happen, though, I needed both of us to be sure of where she stood with this. Pressuring her, or any woman, for that matter, was not on my agenda.

"Benji, if I didn't want to be here, then I wouldn't be. Besides, if I recall correctly, our arrangement includes spending time together, me providing you with a gorgeous date when needed, and you spoiling me rotten in return."

"Very true, but somehow, I don't think tonight counts toward the spoiling-you-rotten requirement."

"I mean, surely orgasms count as spoiling."

Her words had the intended effect, setting my blood on fire and reawakening the hardness between my legs that I'd been trying to keep down. I quickly turned us so that her back was pressed against the balcony railing as my hips ground into her.

"Is that a request or a challenge, Ms. Garner?"

"Sounds like a bit of both to me, Mr. Jordan."

Challenge and request accepted. No more encouragement needed, my hands gripped her waist as I leaned in for a kiss, this one more aggressive than the last. Everything about her made me desperate for her taste in more ways than one, but before I could indulge fully, I wanted to ruin that lipstick again.

She met my intensity with her own, her fingers gripping my button-up so tightly that a hiss escaped me at the feel of her nails. As her tongue stroked against mine, that hiss became a groan that vibrated through my chest.

"You have no idea what that sound does to my pussy," she said, words whispered against my lips.

Fuck. That mouth of hers. "Well, how about we find out?"

My hands turned her, leaving her plump ass nestled right against the hardest part of me. The feel of her left me frozen for a moment, and it was clear that Sage knew exactly what she was doing to me based on the way she pushed even harder, arching her back, so her ass was sitting up in just the right position.

"Why does it feel like you're testing me?" I whispered, nipping at her ear.

"Because I am." Even though I couldn't see her face, I could hear the smile in her voice.

Instead of answering with words, I let my tongue do the talking, allowing it to glide down her neck, flicking against the spots that seemed to make her moan or grind against me. All the while, my fingers made quick work of the thick ribbon crisscrossing along her back until it was bare, the remaining ribbon falling away from her neck.

"Off." The word came out as a growl as I took a step back.

With a coy look over her shoulder, she obliged me, peeling the sequined dress off and stepping out of it seamlessly. The way she looked in the dress was already heart-stopping but standing there with her back to me in nothing but her red thong, I couldn't form a single coherent thought. It took a moment for me to pull myself together.

"Sage, baby, you look so fucking beautiful." As my eyes took in the sight, I moved back in, each hand taking hold of her before tracing my fingers along the edge of the barely-there underwear. "Tell me how beautiful you are."

She may have had every intention of saying it back to me, but instead, a gasp escaped her as my hand dipped below the red material and grazed her drenched lips. The fact that she was already soaking for me turned me on even more. Wasting no time slipping a finger against her clit, I let my teeth graze her shoulder.

"Tell me, baby. I want to hear you say it."

"I-I-I'm so fucking beautiful," she moaned, and it was music to my ears.

I rewarded her by dipping one finger into her, but I swear it felt like I was the one receiving a gift with how hot and wet she was. It only made me want more as my finger sank into her and my thumb slid against the most sensitive piece of her.

"Again."

She let out another gasp as my finger moved in and out of her. "I'm fucking *beautiful*."

The last word came out on a whine as her walls clamped down around me. Her hands gripped the railing as she leaned over, breath coming in pants. I gave her a second finger for listening so well, and this time, her moan was louder.

"You were the most beautiful woman at the party tonight, weren't you?" My fingers pushed into her hard and fast. "*Weren't you?*"

"Yes! God, *yesss*," she hissed as she rolled her hips to meet my strokes.

"They're probably leaving right now. Streaming out of those doors, heading into the streets to go home." I continued fucking her, her pussy getting wetter with each pump of my fingers.

"I wonder if they're looking up here. Do you think they can see the most gorgeous woman they've ever met leaning over the edge of this balcony practically naked while my fingers fuck this perfect little pussy of hers?" My thumb moved faster, and my fingers worked to keep pace. "Think they can see you, baby?"

She whimpered, and I felt her nod.

"You want them to see you, don't you?"

"I do," she gasped, breath catching in her throat as her walls began contracting around my fingers, letting me know that she was close.

"Show everyone how pretty you look when you come." My free hand wrapped around her ponytail as I pulled just hard enough to force her up so that anyone watching really would see her bare chest in all its glory. "Let everyone see my pretty girl come, right now."

My words served as her trigger, those musical moans filling the night air, lifting over the distant sounds coming from the street below. As her walls pulsed around my fingers, the evidence of her orgasm dripped down, soaking my hands and her bare thighs, making a mess of both. It was one of the sexiest things I'd ever witnessed.

"The best girl," I whispered against her hair before letting her ponytail go and sliding down her trembling body until I was eye-to-eye with the only place I wanted to be right now.

My fingers slipped free, and I brought them to my lips, sucking them clean and groaning at her taste. It was just as delicious as I'd imagined, but it wasn't enough. I wanted it straight from the source.

"Bend over and spread those thick thighs for me, Sweetness. It's time for me to have a real taste."

8

SAGE

"Oh my—"

The words weren't even out before I was hit with another tremor, and a high-pitched squeal left my lips. My grip on the balcony railing tightened as I pushed myself back further into Benjamin's mouth. If it wasn't for the strong grip his hands had on me, there was no doubt in my mind that my weak ass knees would've had me on the floor.

His slurping sounds turned me on even more, and I was sure he was tasting the proof of that. I'd always wondered what Benjamin would be like if we ever ended up in this situation. A laugh bubbled up in my throat at the thought because I'd been sure he'd be soft and sweet. Borderline proper. I never could have imagined that he'd be my favorite type of nasty. The type to bend and fuck me with his tongue from the back, outside where anyone could hear or see us, while telling me that I had the prettiest pussy he'd ever seen. Was this what fucking with older men was like? If it was, then I'd truly been missing out.

His nails dug into my skin as they moved down to spread my ass open for him to give him a better view of what was behind my already swollen lower lips. He was toying with me, driving me out of my mind. Every time my second orgasm started to rise, he would pull back. Every lick, every groan he let loose, every one of his ministrations pushed me closer and closer to the edge, but he refused to let me tip over.

"Benji, *pleeease*," I whined, pouting as I rode the three fingers he'd begun fucking me with. "I'm s-s-so clo —*oooh*..." The cool air he blew against my exposed pussy sent shivers down my spine.

"I love you like this."

Lick.

Somehow, I managed to answer between pants. "Like what? A begging mess?"

Slurp.

"Yes," he chuckled before he replaced his fingers with his tongue, dipping it into me.

Why the hell did that feel so good?

"But it's more than that," he added when he finally pulled away, once again denying me the orgasm I desperately needed.

"You're like a goddamn painting, baby. One that should be worshiped, witnessed, and admired over and over again."

I tucked my bottom lip between my teeth as I widened my stance to give him better access. His thumb strummed my clit, and I felt the urge to beg again.

Thank God I didn't have to. As hard as he worked to keep me from falling off the edge before, he was working double time to push me straight over the cliff now. Those amazing lips wrapped around my clit as he licked and sucked like his life depended on it. I was crying, *shit, I was crying*, but as wild as it sounded, I couldn't help myself. The way his tongue twirled around my sweet spot just felt so *fucking* satisfying.

With him still on his knees behind me, his hand began to move, and before I could even register what was happening, his thumb, which was covered in my juices, was trying to push into the space where no one else had ever been. As it slipped in, the moan I let out could only be described as primal.

"Benji, yes. Oh *FUCK, YES*," I called out, grinding and dripping all over his face. If the groans he was making were any indication, he was loving every minute of this just as much as I was, not wanting to waste a drop.

I was flying towards orgasm number three, and it was there before I could blink, not even giving me a moment to catch my breath. This time, my knees really did give out, and Benjamin didn't miss a beat, twisting onto his back and bringing me down to sit on his face. I was a whimpering mess and knew somebody could probably hear me, but I didn't give one good goddamn.

"Stop, I ca—" The full words wouldn't come, so instead, I tried to slide away from his mouth. He resisted at first but finally gave in, letting me move back until I was sitting on his chest instead, gasping for air.

We stayed that way, both of us trying to catch our breath as the sounds of the city down below finally began to filter back in. It was hard to miss the way his face glistened with the mess he'd pulled from me. The overhead lighting only made it more obvious. His smile was clear as day, and that brought a smile to my face. After taking it all in, we both burst out laughing.

"I cannot believe we just did that," I said, leaning over so our bodies lined up and my face hovered above his.

"Which part? The one where I ate that unbelievably beautiful pussy until you screamed loud enough to be heard across town or the one where you squirted all over my face right out in the open on this balcony?"

"Mmmm, let's go with both." My lips connected with his, and the fact that I could taste myself there had me grinding against him again.

"I think your shirt might be ruined...maybe the pants too," I gasped into his mouth. He thrust upward, letting me feel just how ready he was.

"I'll buy new ones. Or maybe I'll save 'em because this is a night I'm going to constantly want to relive in my mind." He traced his fingers along my cheek, and I nuzzled against them, loving how appreciated the entire moment made me feel.

"Are you saying we're done? Need to tap out already? I would hate to wear you out at your age."

My tone was teasing, but the fire in his eyes wasn't. "I'm nowhere near done with you. Go ahead and take your pretty ass over to the bed. *Now.*"

The last word had so much force behind it that it felt like a shot of adrenaline. I arched my eyebrows and giggled, doing exactly as he instructed.

Since he hadn't told me how he wanted me on the bed, my own desires took over, and I climbed on top ass in the air, a perfect arch in my back. Sending a teasing look over my shoulder, I watched as he walked toward me. With each step, he took off another piece of clothing. His shoes. His shirt. The belt. Those pants that made his ass look unreal. They all came off one by one, and suddenly I was the one mesmerized by his beauty.

"I didn't realize a striptease was on the menu tonight."

That pulled a chuckle out of him as he finally made it to the bed, just as his boxers hit the floor. "I didn't realize *you* were on the menu tonight. Sounds like we both found ourselves pleasantly surprised."

Focusing on whatever he was saying was out of the question because the only thing that I could pay attention to was the certified monster between his legs. It was the adoration in his next words that broke the spell.

"I wish you could see the way you look right now. Baby, you belong in a museum. People should have to pay for the privilege to lay eyes on you."

The slight irony of his statement wasn't lost on me, and any other time I would point it out, but the way he spoke those words as his hand wrapped around his thick shaft...there was only one thing that needed to be said.

"Shut up, Benji, and fuck me like I deserve it."

If I thought that would get a rise out of him, it didn't. He only smiled and made quick work of sheathing himself in a condom, happy to hear me talking my shit. "Don't worry, baby. I plan on it."

A shriek left me as he flipped me over and yanked me

by the ankles, pulling me closer to the edge of the bed. "But I want to look into those beautiful eyes while I do it."

I didn't think I could get any wetter, but he was doing his damnedest to prove me wrong. How could he make something so sweet sound so...filthy? To find out that Benji had been hiding this very particular set of skills from me made me kind of upset.

That feeling disappeared as soon as I felt his hard, thick shaft slide between my legs. Every pass over my clit drew a whimper out of me, and my hunger only grew once I realized he was coating himself in my desire. Watching the way his eyes lit up as he did it and hearing the resulting moan he let out let me know we both wanted more.

The first stroke was toe-curling, and that wasn't an exaggeration. My toes were literally gripping the plush comforter as my back bowed and he worked to get fully seated inside of me. My eyes fluttered shut as the sound of him mumbling reached my ears, and the only words I could make out were "warm" and "wet."

"Are you ready, Sweetness? Please tell me you're ready?" he asked, voice strained.

"*Sooo* ready." My hips moved of their own accord, tired of waiting. He was stretching me in a way that I didn't think possible, but the slight pain only heightened my pleasure. Benjamin followed my lead, sliding out of me before thrusting back in, each stroke hitting deeper than the last.

The way he was fucking me felt better than anything

I'd ever experienced in my life. Our bodies were so in tune, rising and falling in a way that complemented each other. My fingers found their way to my nipple, pulling and twisting until I couldn't help but cup my entire breast in my hand to bring it up to my mouth. My tongue flicked out to meet it, the slightly rough surface making the hardened peak that much more sensitive.

"That's right, baby," Benji grunted as his eyes took in the sight. "Show me what you like. Show me what gets you off."

That bit of encouragement was all I needed, and soon I was pulling that same nipple into my mouth completely, sucking and toying with it even more. I moaned around myself as I closed my eyes, turned on not only by my actions but how I must look while doing it. I was so captivated by the sensation that I missed the moment when he leaned forward on his forearms, pulling my neglected nipple into his mouth.

I let loose a keening sound as his strokes sped up, and his tongue worried my nipple more insistently. I tried to pull him in as close as I could, one hand on the back of his head, holding him to my chest as the nails of my other hand scraped at his back. How was he filling me so completely? There was no part of me that he left untouched. I pulled his head up, guiding him to my lips for a kiss, but instead, he gifted me with words of praise.

"You feel so good, Sage, baby."

"You deserve this dick. Fuck, you deserve it."

"I'll never get tired of this pussy. It's magical, Sweetness."

Each word sent a shock through my system, and my moans became uncontrollable cries.

"Can I play with that clit, baby? I want to feel you wet up this dick like you wet up my face. You did such a good fucking job."

"*SHIIIT!*" I sobbed, nodding quickly, craving what he was offering.

His hand snaked between us, and his thumb went to work as his body pulled away from mine until only our lower halves met. "*So* good at it. Show me how exceptional you are." His free hand bent my leg and held it down until I was spread out before him, completely bare and exposed.

"I said show me, Sage!" he barked, the groan that followed almost as deep as the stroke he was fucking me with. My body seized up, and my mouth fell open on a silent scream as my eyes watered up again.

God, he was giving me another release that brought me to tears. His ass was fucking dangerous. His mouth, his words, his dick. They were mind-altering. Life-changing. I should be running for the hills because this was the sort of sex that destroyed lives, but instead, I embraced every bit of it as I let go, leaving him practically drowning in my release before it forced him out and soaked the sheets underneath me.

By the time he flipped me over and thrust back in, I couldn't do anything beyond take every inch of him as his pace quickened, apparently determined to pull another nut out of me. I don't know how long we carried on like that, switching positions again and again, my strength ebbing and flowing. It could have been minutes. Possibly hours. All I knew was that as Benji came inside me and groaned my name sometime later, my legs almost behind my head and my breath caught in my throat, I would never look at this man the same. *Never.*

9

BENJAMIN

"Sage, baby."

My words were met with a frustrated whine, causing me to laugh. An idea formed in my head as I stood over her. The sight of her laying on her stomach, not a stitch of clothing on, was enough for me to begin to stiffen again, but I willed myself to calm down.

Her ass sitting up perfectly did give me the opportunity to do something else, though. Without another thought, my hand came down in a smack that cracked through the room. Sage let out a small shriek and turned around, shooting me an irritated look.

"Benji, what the hell?!"

Leaning over to place a kiss on the spot that had taken the brunt of my hit, I said, "Had to come up with some way to get your attention and get you moving. Unless you've changed your mind about sleeping in the wet spot."

She huffed, finally sitting up with a pout. "But I'm tired! Your old ass wore me out."

This time the laugh that came out of me was full-bodied. "That's quite a bit of audacity for a woman who was ready to tap out twenty minutes ago."

"Only to give my very mature, very skilled partner a break," she teased. Getting to her feet, she wrapped her arms around my neck. "I thought I was being considerate."

"Mhmm," I chuckled. "Well, take your very considerate ass on and freshen up."

"Hate to break it to you, baby, but neither one of us has stuff here, and it's literally a brand new, unopened hotel. I'm not sure there's anything to freshen up with or sheets to switch."

"Don't be so sure."

I pulled away and gestured for her to follow me into the front room of the suite. She had no idea, but Philip had equipped the rooms with all the necessities that his guests would need once he realized that most of us would probably not make it home for one reason or another. A basket of fresh linens, hygiene products, and robes were situated on the coffee table in the living room area.

"Very sneaky," she said, grabbing a plush robe.

"More like very prepared," I said before explaining how the items had arrived. While she was drifting off to sleep, I may have asked to have a few extra amenities that Sage was partial to sent up, but I didn't see a point in mentioning it. Making sure she was taken care of was second nature to me. This was just another aspect of that.

"Now, why don't you go and judge the water pressure in the rain shower while I put fresh sheets on the bed?"

"Thank you, Benji." After gifting me with a quick kiss, she headed toward the master bath, and I used that time to do exactly what I said. Once I finished, I grabbed my things and headed to the second bathroom to follow my own advice. By the time that was done, Sage was already in bed waiting for me.

"You know you could've just showered with me," she said with a raised eyebrow.

"Something tells me that at least one of us would've gotten just a bit too distracted if I'd made that decision."

She winked before saying, "Maybe," patting the space next to her.

Once I settled in, admittedly a bit too comfortable with the way she felt lying against my chest, a quiet settled over us. Now that everything had calmed down and the adrenaline was gone, I was left with my own thoughts. I'd imagined being with Sage like this more times than I cared to admit. My imagination hadn't even come close to reality. The taste of her, the feel of her, the smell of her...all of it was otherworldly. How would I go back to our original way of being now that I'd been introduced to the other side?

"This was certainly...*not* how I expected the night to go when I accepted your invitation," Sage said as she traced her fingers along my chest underneath the white robe.

"Me either." I paused. "I know this isn't our usual..." My sentence trailed off before starting again. "I don't want you to think that..."

After pausing again, I took a deep breath.

That gave her the time to sit up and look at me a little too gleefully.

"Benjamin Jordan, are you nervous?" she gasped.

"Nervous? No. Unsure of what to say? Yes." Maybe I should've been embarrassed to admit that, but as a grown man, I had no problem being vulnerable in this situation.

"Unsure *because...*"

"Because this is new for us. I know what you agreed to a year ago, Sage, and I don't want you to think I'll expect something different from you now."

"First of all, let's not act like I didn't want this to happen just as much as you did, Benjamin." If she was using my full name, I knew she had to be serious. "I'm an adult, and I make my own decisions. If you don't know anything about me after this past year, I would hope you know that no one can make me do anything that I don't want to."

I nodded in understanding. "I do know that, and I'm not saying anything to the contrary."

"Good." Placing a kiss on my lips, she continued. "Benji, I know you're used to having everything planned out and handled, but tonight doesn't have to be anything other than what it is right now. Let's just enjoy it, no promises, no complications, no expectations."

Admittedly, her ability to get me out of my own head was one of the things that I loved about Sage. She was right. Sometimes it was difficult for me to deal with the unknown. That was one of the reasons I made sure the terms of our agreement were crystal clear from the beginning.

"Besides, didn't we already agree that orgasms count as spoiling?"

"Is that what we agreed?"

"Let's just say I'm officially making that amendment...for now."

"Well then, I guess I'd better get to work."

I'd had every intention of removing her robe, but from the way she slid down my body and unbelted mine, it was clear she had different plans.

"Uh-uh. It's my turn to do a bit of spoiling."

There were no words to describe how stunning Sage looked as she wrapped her hand around my shaft. Between the way her nails looked surrounding me and how she hungrily licked her lips, I couldn't be sure which was causing my dick to jump or leak precum. *Shit*, I was pretty sure it didn't matter, especially once her tongue flicked out across my slit. A moan immediately left me as I pressed my head back into the pillow.

"Good God."

"Not God, Benji. Just Sage," she said before those gorgeous lips pulled me into her mouth, and she flattened her tongue against the underside of my shaft.

I was lost to the sensation, and once Sage was done showing me how talented she was with her mouth, she climbed on top of me and demonstrated just how beautiful my baby could be as she rode me into the next morning.

10

SAGE

THE WAY THE SUN WAS STREAMING INTO THE bedroom had me regretting the decision not to engage the blackout curtains as Benjamin had suggested. As his name skittered across my thoughts, I turned, my morning brain fog trying to figure out why I didn't feel his warm body next to mine. He had to be just as worn out as I was after fucking each other senseless well into the early morning.

It took a moment, but I finally zeroed in on the small sheet of paper that had taken his place in bed.

Unfortunately, I was called into the office this morning for an emergency investor meeting. No need to rush home. Sleep in and then have whatever you want delivered to the room. Philip's chef and staff are preparing brunch for anyone who

decided to stay overnight. Francis will be there to pick you up whenever you're ready.
-Benjamin

Pouting, I stretched, surprised to find myself just a bit annoyed at waking up alone. Meals with Benji were always something I looked forward to—especially, it seemed, when I knew there was a possibility that I might be on the menu.

Instead of letting the discovery ruin my mood, I took his instructions to heart and called downstairs to order something to eat. After hearing everything available for the morning, I decided to order a few things, including blueberry waffles, eggs Benedict topped with lobster, candied maple bacon, and some mimosas. Our two-person workout had left me starving. Once that was taken care of, I snuggled back up in bed. Resisting the urge to send a text message was more difficult than I'd originally thought, but if Benjamin was in an important meeting, then the last thing I wanted to do was disturb him.

It wasn't hard to busy myself with social media until a knock at the door sounded, letting me know that the food had arrived. I quickly tossed on my robe and went to collect it. What I hadn't been expecting was the gorgeous Chanel overnight bag that came with my meal.

"Compliments of Mr. Jordan. He gave specific instructions to have it delivered with your brunch."

I thanked the bellhop quickly and offered to tip him, but of course, that had already been taken care of as well.

The smell of the food overrode my curiosity about what was in the bag, so I dug in without a second thought. Once I was finally too full to take another bite, I took a peek at what goodies Benji had sent my way. A squeal left me at the sight of the designer outfit, complete with shoes, in the bag, along with a note.

As beautiful as you looked in last night's dress, I figured you'd appreciate a more appropriate going-home outfit.

And he was absolutely right. I was in no rush to head back home, though, so instead, I took a long, luxurious soak in the bathtub before moisturizing with the different products that Benjamin provided. I would definitely need to make a hair appointment considering how much he'd enjoyed pulling mine all night, so I took care of that as well. In the meantime, a messy bun would have to do.

By the time Fran confirmed he was on his way, I was thoroughly relaxed, pampered, and satisfied. The only thing missing was the man who'd worked to make it happen. Snapping a quick picture to send him once I was dressed, I typed out:

> Thank you, Benji. Everything was perfect.

His response was almost instant.

BENJAMIN:

> No, perfect would have been being able to sleep in with you and then wake you and that pretty pussy up with my face between your legs.
> Looks like I'll have to try again next time.

Rubbing my thighs together to relieve some of the pressure his statement created, I went to reply, only to be interrupted by a call letting me know that Fran was here, as promised, to take me home. I grabbed my new bag filled with everything from the night before and the robe I was now officially claiming as mine and made my way out of the room to the elevator to head downstairs. On the way, I typed out my response.

> What happened to 'just for last night'?

BENJAMIN:

> It went out the window sometime around 3 AM. Flew right over the balcony. You didn't see it?

My laughter filled the elevator just as it came to a stop. Fran was in the lobby waiting for me and took my bag before escorting me to the car.

> So what are you saying?

BENJAMIN:

> I'm saying maybe that amendment of yours could be taken into consideration again. Just for one more night.

Only one more night? If I had any say in it, we'd be getting more than that. But in the meantime...

I think that could be arranged.

"Did you enjoy yourself, Ms. Garner?" Fran asked once we were settled in our respective places in the town car.

The smile on my face refused to disappear, but that was fine with me. "In ways that I never expected."

A FINAL WORD

I hope you enjoyed meeting Sage and Benjamin as much as I enjoyed introducing them to you. These two burst onto the scene with no notice, but I had such a great time with them. If you feel the same way, please consider leaving a rating and/or review on your favorite platform (Amazon, Goodreads, Storygraph, etc.) They're the best way to help readers find new favorites and are so important in terms of indie author support.

To keep up-to-date on upcoming Lady Marie projects, be sure to sign up for the Spice In Your Life Newsletter, join me on Patreon (Lady Marie Affair), check out my linktree, and follow me on social media @ladymariewrites.

To order a signed copy of any of my paperback projects, merch, or web exclusives, please visit the Lady Marie Shop at www.ladymariewrites.com

And don't worry. The Sugared and Spiced universe is just getting started.

ACKNOWLEDGMENTS

Every single bit of thanks to Ashley, Tanon, and Kai. This project was both unexpected and (mostly) unplanned, but the three of you didn't hesitate to jump on this random journey with me. Always locked in and zero switch ups. Love y'all for that.

ALSO BY LADY MARIE